Do You Know How to Grow?

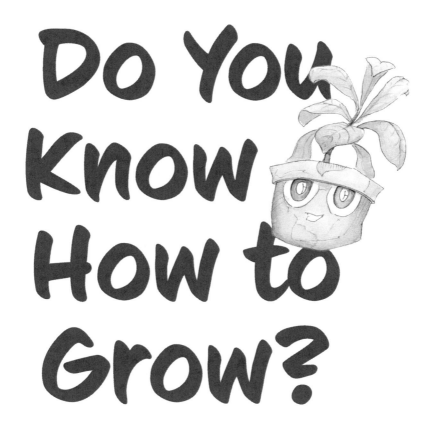

By Brian Atchue

Illustrated by David Fox

Designed by Nicole Powdar

@hanginghouseplants

ISBN: 9798546130336

First and foremost thank you to you! I would not be writing a children's book without the supportive community of plant lovers who changed my life forever. I hope you love the book!

Thank you to my wife Leila and my son Kai. I am truly blessed to be in love with my best friend and starting a beautiful family together. I can't wait to read you this book Kai. I hope the message resonates with you as you grow.

Thank you to my family for always being the greatest support team anyone could wish for. My family has always believed in me even when I've had doubts, and I would be nowhere without them.

Thank you to Nicole Powdar for her creative direction designing the layout of this book. Who knew two desk mates talking about movies would someday collaborate on children's book! I am very thankful for our friendship.

Thank you to Mohammad Qabbani for his photography and editing of the paintings. We've been making it up as we go through this entire process and you helped us capture Dave's stunning paintings and helped this train keep rolling.

Finally thank you to David Fox. Dave is one of my oldest friends whose talents are limitless. Someone that can accomplish anything when he's focused and passionate. A truly gifted artist who I'm thrilled to have collaborated on this book with. I'm so excited for the world to see what he can do.

There once
was a little fig,

Who dreamt
of growing big.

There was one
problem though,

It didn't know
how to grow.

Fig wished it
knew what to do,
but it didn't have a clue.

6

Oh, I know!

I'll ask some other
plants how to grow!

Fig climbed up until,
Its pot was safely
on the sill.

Hi,
I'm Cacti!

I'm Fig and want
to grow big!

Do you know
how to grow?

Of course,
little one.

The secret's
lots of sun!

Fig soaked in lots of light.

But something wasn't right.

This light was way too bright!

13

I think I need a drink,

My leaves have started to shrink.

No you don't,
you'll be fine,

I don't like water
and look at mine.

Fig found
a corner
with lots
of shade,

A fern was
there who
came to
its aid.

I'm Fig and want to grow big!

Do you know how to grow?

Hello I'm Fern,
And yes,
would you like to learn?

That sounds
great, I'll
give it a try,

I won't let
my soil ever
get dry.

Fig drank water all day long,

Once again something was wrong.

Fig wasn't
feeling so good,

Is there something
Fig misunderstood?

Then a snake plant came along,

And asked, "Little plant, what is wrong?"

27

I'm Fig and want
to grow big!

But now I think
I need a wig!

I've asked so many plants what to do,

But none of them seem to have a clue!

One said
more light,
the other
said less,

Does anyone know or
do they just guess!

Everything
you learned
was true,

You just
haven't found
what's right
for you!

Some plants drink water everyday,

Some plants say keep that stuff away.

We all need different
types of care,

We come
from all over,
both here and there.

Being different doesn't
make you weak,

It makes you special –
we're all unique!

Don't try and grow too fast, there's no rush

Before you know it, your leaves will be lush.

38

Get some
light but not
too much,

Drink water when your
soil's dry to the touch.

Thank you
for all
the advice,

Taking my time
sounds very nice.

Fig went
and found the
perfect spot,

Some light, some water,
and not too hot!

After some time wouldn't you know,

Fig finally learned how to grow.

The
End